FAITHFUL TO THE CAUSE

by
Julianne S. Condrey

Royal Fireworks Press
Unionville, New York
Toronto, Ontario

To my family, especially Douglas, thanks for the encouragement and to S. Douglas Fleet, who shares my love of Walkerton with special thanks to the staff at Meadow Farm Museum and to Gloria, for your efforts.

Copyright © 1998, R Fireworks Publishing Company, Ltd.
All Rights Reserved.

Royal Fireworks Press
First Avenue, PO Box 399
Unionville, NY 10988-0399
(914) 726-4444
FAX: (914) 726-3824
email: rfpress@frontiernet.net

Royal Fireworks Press
78 Biddeford Avenue
Downsview, Ontario
M3H 1K4 Canada
FAX: (416) 633-3010

ISBN: 0-88092-403-9

Printed in the United States of America using vegetable-based inks on acid-free, recycled paper by the Royal Fireworks Printing Co. of Unionville, New York.

CHAPTER 1

Sarah sipped her tea absentmindedly as she looked out beyond the covered porch onto Grace Street. All of Richmond was alive that warm April afternoon. She let her eyes wander up and down the busy street as she listened to her cousin go on in her rhythmic voice.

"Oh, let them fool Yankee barbarians come and try to tell our Southern gentlemen what to do. They'll be runnin' back home with their tails between their legs before long!" Felicity said with a giggle as she imagined the Yankee humiliation. Her long, auburn hair tumbled down in ringlets where it had escaped the crocheted hairnet. Pink flooded her cheeks as she spoke with enthusiasm.

Her piercing green eyes make her such a lovely creature, Sarah thought, admiring her cousin as she had done since they were small girls. A gentle breeze stirred up the white damask tablecloth that draped the porch table where they enjoyed their afternoon tea. "Yes, they'll be sorry, but it won't be pleasant, war that is, for either side, I'm sure. I was reading about the War of Independence..." Sarah began, her blue eyes concentrating on a group of children across the street.

"Dear, you read too much and worry even more. You are quite like your mother at times, Sarah. You must behave like the sixteen-year-old lovely that you are! Let us rejoice, for surely Virginia will secede now that South Carolina has captured Fort Sumter. Friday, April the twelfth, 1861 will be remembered as the start of something great!"

Felicity always has such a carefree attitude toward serious matters, Sarah thought. Inwardly disagreeing she was at all like her mother, she nibbled on the lemon tea cakes just brought out to the ladies. Sarah felt the excitement of spring, of events yet to be. Yet her spirit felt a foreboding fire not even Felicity could quench. Sarah looked again at the young children across the road. She heard them taunting, saying ugly things to Miss Van Lew as the dark-haired woman stood proudly ignoring their vain threats.

"Some say she's a Union woman, but she is quite pleasant company, I must say. Her Northern education has made her quite the advanced woman," Felicity said when she noticed Sarah's concern. "Come, let's take part in the celebration!" Felicity danced indoors to the piano, giddy with delight. She was barely seated when "Dixie" began to pour from her graceful fingertips. When Felicity played, her whole being came alive, and she entered a realm Sarah yearned to take part in, one of complete harmony. Felicity's thin, noble face would flush with excitement as her fingertips danced from key to key pouring out sounds of angels on high. She played louder to compete with the crowd parading down the street with the band. Sarah longed to be so gifted at something that life would flow like a gentle stream, pure and unbroken.

Sarah caught a glimpse of herself in the round mirror above the piano. Her blond hair neatly parted in the center and pulled so smooth and tight as only Peachy could do so well. Peachy was Sarah's favorite servant and always accompanied Sarah to visit her cousin. Sarah's deep blue dress looked fresh and smart despite the newly acquired tea stain on the front. Her blue eyes sparkled on her fair, round face that afternoon as she prepared for the unknown. Suddenly, the music crashed to a stop.

"Insolent girl, find your place please!" Felicity hissed as Peachy, drawn to the excitement, worked her way to the piano bench beside Felicity. Peachy drew back in respect of Felicity, but her pride was unbroken and her face remained calm. Felicity's eyes narrowed as she waited for Sarah to correct Peachy.

Sarah said quietly, "Apologize to Miss Felicity, Peachy."

"Miss Felicity, ma'am, I's sorry, and I will be more careful," Peachy said firmly but without malice. Her medium complexion revealed a rosiness in her cheeks as she confronted Felicity. Sarah noticed the rage in Felicity's eyes and the peaceful, sober look on Peachy's face.

"Foolish darkies, we must keep them in their place, Sarah, or they'll be out of control. Even the ones we consider faithful to us will run or stab us in our sleep if we don't remind them of their standing. Remember what happened to Charlotte Jones? They stabbed her and left her for dead before they ran," Felicity half-whispered after Peachy had retreated to the safety of the kitchen.

"I believe in treating all humans, black or white, with decency."

"There is nothing decent about a savage or inferior."

Quickly, Sarah turned the conversation. "I am so glad I was able to visit and enjoy your party, dear Cousin. If I didn't have such a terribly long ride home, I'm quite certain you could persuade me to linger on your porch and share all the tasty news of Julia's new beau and whatever else you've managed to squeeze out of our friends!" Sarah pressed her hands into her cousin's.

"I have yet to find out about the mysterious Alex you are so fond of. Maybe next time I can plan to torture you with senseless riddles, until you beg me to stop, so that you can pour out your heart to your dear cousin. But until then, I will be content knowing that I know as much or more than anyone else about the elusive Alexander," Felicity laughed. "I do hope we can be together again soon. By then perhaps this silly war will be over and Virginia will be a triumphant part of the Confederate nation."

Blushing as she always did at the mention of Alex, Sarah was grateful Felicity didn't press further about the matter. "Yes, of course. Oh, Uncle Thomas, thank you so much for the lovely time. You will give my love to Aunt Maria, won't you?" Sarah said to the hazel-eyed gentleman as he entered the parlor. His graceful build and auburn hair resembled Sarah's mother so much it made him even more special.

"Sweet child, give our love to your mother and father and the children. I hope they will be as excited about the news as we are." Uncle Thomas smiled as he pointed to a small Confederate flag proudly standing on the piano.

With a kiss on either cheek of her mother's favorite brother and a quick embrace with Felicity, Sarah made her way down the front steps, trailed by Peachy with their bags. Sarah entered the coach with wide eyes as people walked past shouting loudly, each trying to outdo the next. "Let's join the others in the Cause!" some would say. With a final wave to Uncle Thomas and Felicity, Sarah took a final glance at the stately home across the road from them where Miss Van Lew soberly stared out her parlor window.

In all of her trips to Richmond, Sarah had never seen the people so utterly intoxicated with purpose. Cannon fire in the distance punctuated the shouts. Josiah steered the horses down Franklin to cross Shockoe Creek. As the Capitol came into view, throngs of people stood waiting to hear Governor Letcher speak. Peachy prodded Sarah. "Miss Sarah, look at those two chillins up on the roof, they's gonna kill themselves," Peachy said disapprovingly as two young boys attempted to replace the Stars and Stripes with a Confederate flag. The crowd seemed to gasp in unison as one of the boys tumbled down the roof of the building. Sarah clutched Peachy's arm as they watched the boy's firm-footed accomplice stop his fall. Relief was expresed as a collective sigh across the capitol grounds. As excited citizens saluted the accomplishment of their South Carolinian friends and heralded the unavoidable secession of Virginia, gunshots echoed throughout the area.

"Peachy, I do believe the people of Richmond have gone mad," Sarah said with her mouth remaining open in disbelief.

"Yes'm," Peachy said with a smile.

Sarah gasped as a young man thrust his head through the open window of the stationary coach. "Ladies, won't you stay and join in this wondrous celebration?" he said. His eyes were wild with excitement and the smell of liquor permeated the air. Sarah's pocketbook landed with a smack on his face as she screamed, "Josiah!" The stunned man pulled his head back quickly and returned to boistrous street revelry as Sarah leaned out the window and yelled above the noise, "Josiah, let's avoid further crowds and hurry onto Brook Avenue. The faster we leave Richmond, the safer I will feel." Leaning back on the black velvet cushions, Sarah sighed as the coach started forward again.

The farther north from the city they travelled, the farther apart houses became. Farmers fields and woods now graced the scenery. "There is such a comfortable feeling out here away form the noise and confusion of the city, isn't there, Peachy?" Sarah spoke very personally and openly with Peachy, as she had always done, on their trips together. Peachy looked up from her reading, *Pride and Prejudice*, and Sarah remembered how the two of them conspired to teach Peachy how to read in spite of the severe penalties discovery would bring.

"Yes'm, mighty peaceful. More and more I prefer the country over the wonders of the city."

Sarah nodded her agreement as Peachy continued with her reading. She tried hard not to laugh at the puzzled expression on Peachy's face as she reacted to the goings on in Jane Austen's novel.

Pulling a worn envelope from her pocketbook, Sarah unfolded the letter it contained and began to read the words she had memorized during the last few weeks.

My Dearest Sarah,

It has only been a month since our last visit together, yet it feels as if an entire year has exhausted itself. I can see your lovely, fair face and sparkling blue eyes every time I close my eyes for but a moment. If you only knew how much I take pleasure in your company.

My petite love, I value and cherish you. My intentions are for marriage, as I have discussed with your Father. If you care for me, as I do you, we shall be ever so happy together. I long to be near you again.

Lovingly yours,
Corporal Alexander Brooke

Sarah breathed in deeply and closed her eyes, imagining Alex's thick, chestnut hair, and his intense brown eyes staring into hers. She felt his strong grip on her arm as they walked through the garden together before he returned to the Virginia Military Institute. *He loves me! How wonderful life can be!* she thought.

Sarah was shaken from her reverie as the coach pulled up beside the brick pillars and iron gates that marked the entrance to the Wright family farm. Although Sarah had enjoyed her week in Richmond with Felicity, she longed to see her family again. "Papa!" Sarah shouted as she hopped out of the coach and ran to her father's side.

"My Sarah, did you enjoy your cousin's party and all your girlish fun?" Papa grinned as he swept Sarah up in his arms for a bear hug.

"Oh, yes, but I've missed you all. Has it been busy here? Many patients?"

"A true nurse to the center of your being. No, it's been a slow week. But, an exciting day. I've heard the news of Fort Sumter. I trust our country pace will be disrupted soon if Virginia chooses to join the Confederacy, which more than likely she will." Sarah couldn't help but notice the disappointment in his voice.

Sarah walked beside her father toward the three-story brick great house. The double front porch and white pillars were freshly whitewashed and seemed to shine in the springtime sun. The orange-red bricks revealed the color of the local soil and craftsmanship. Sarah noticed the drawing room curtains flutter and then her mother appeared at the doorway with Julia and Carter hanging on her bright yellow skirt. Her fair skin contrasted with her auburn hair which was, as usual, parted in the center and held in a chignon at the base of her neck. Sarah loved it when her mother would let that wondrous mane tumble down to her waist and surround her graceful frame like a silky cape as she brushed it each evening.

Sarah bounded up the fifteen porch steps and gave her mother a quick kiss on either cheek.

"Sarah, mind you are a lady! It's so good to have you home! Peachy, see to her bath shortly, she looks worn and rumpled. How are Uncle Thomas and Aunt Maria?" Mrs. Wright spoke so quickly she barely gave Sarah a chance to respond.

8

But Sarah saw the worry etched in her mother's face as she pulled back. "What is it, Mother?" Sarah lovingly held her mother's arm.

"Oh, just this silly talk of war. Not to worry, dear." Her mother smiled tenderly. "Corporal Brooke left word that he'll be joining us Wednesday for dinner. Such a fine, young man." Mrs. Wright glanced knowingly at Sarah to see her reaction to her beloved's name. Sarah was so young and naive about men callers, this was how it should be, Dr. and Mrs. Wright agreed. No need for a different beau each month. Find a good, Christian man and stick with him.

Sarah blushed. "Did he ask about me while I was in Richmond?"

Mrs. Wright looked at Sarah and then returned her watchful gaze to Julia and Carter playing with the cat. "Yes, he did," she said simply.

Knowing her mother's reserve, Sarah satisfied herself with the fact Alex had merely mentioned her name. She hummed quietly in time with the cat's swishing tail.

CHAPTER 2

Wednesday seemed to take weeks to arrive instead of days. When the day finally dawned, it brought a messenger galloping up the drive for Papa.

"Dr. Wright, it's for certain. Virginia has joined the Confederacy. Strength to the Cause!" The youngster gave a holler as he tipped his hat to Sarah who was reading on the porch.

Dr. Wright turned slowly toward his wife as the young bearer of monumental tidings rode off to his next destination. Mrs. Wright saw an aging man before her as he weakly replied, "Elizabeth, did you ever think war would come to our wonderful land?" With that, he trudged to his office at the rear of the house.

"Mr. Brooke still joining us for dinner, Miss Lizbeth?" Mary's strong voice approached from behind Mrs. Wright.

Mary, although cheerful in countenance and strong in body, still bore the appearance of many years in servitude. The scar on her right cheek served as a reminder of her previous owner's anger at a runaway attempt. Fearless and strong, Mary would have tried again to be reunited with her husband Peter and daughter Peachy who had been sold to Dr. Wright. But Dr. Wright learned of the family's separation, and returned to Timber Creek and purchased Mary. "No need in selling off their family, no more than I'd see fit to sell my own," he would reply to potential buyers.

"Yes, please see to his needs when he arrives, Mary," Mrs. Wright replied faintly as she stared at her husband entering his office.

Being a country doctor was quite different from working in the city. Dr. Wright's education gave him the privilege of being a local magistrate as well. Between his practice and handling other people's affairs, Dr. Wright spent most of his time in his office or riding to different farms in the area to tend to sick folks. That, of course, required an additional charge to the patient, but Dr. Wright's charitable nature got the better of him, and often he accepted gifts in place of payment. Of course, Mrs. Wright's displeasure of sick folks so near her children made her grateful the office was not in the house.

"Oh, here comes another patient now," Mrs. Wright said with a yawn.

The rider whistled melodically and Sarah jumped. She tried not to appear too anxious as she made her way down the front steps, but she couldn't stop her legs from breaking into a run toward the handsome, young man whose fashionable dress and fair, thin face gave him an elegant appearance. His strength of character was matched by his physical carriage, which made him the ideal instructor at the Virginia Military Institute. Alex swung off the saddle to Sarah's side. "Whoa, young lady!" he said, smiling broadly as he took both of Sarah's hands in his. "Grace was in all her steps, heav'n in her eye, in every gesture dignity and love," Alex quoted. He bowed and kissed the hands of his fair lady.

"Oh, Alex you are too sweet to me," Sarah breathed.

"One could never be too sweet for you my love. Have you heard the good news?"

"If you are referring to our secession, then yes, I have."

"Why do you not look pleased? Surely you can't help but rejoice that Virginia will triumph over those who seek to destroy our way of life?"

"I'm just sad at the prospect of you going to war, Alex," Sarah reasoned.

"Do not fret your beautiful little head, my dear. This war will be over before it's hardly begun. Now, enough of such talk, let's join the others inside."

The smell of freshly washed and oiled pine floors was masked by the aromas drifting out of the kitchen. The portrait of George Washington in the center hall presided over the various preparations as it had certainly done since the house was built almost thirty years earlier for use as a tavern. A large, crystal chandelier graced the mahogany railed stairway that ascended to the third floor.

"Mary has prepared a meal fit for celebration. Ham and turnip greens, turkey, hominy, rice, sweet potatoes, baked and fried shad and oyster soup," Sarah said excitedly.

"I do always enjoy eating here at the farm."

Alex seated Mrs. Wright and then Sarah at the well polished dining table.

"Yes, but I still prefer the ice cream, cakes and jellies when the meal is through," Prescott added as he jumped down the last few stairs. His hazel eyes and thin build were reminiscent of Uncle Thomas.

"A boy of thirteen seldom doesn't like the sweet things in life," Alex mischievously replied.

"Especially sweet things named Victoria!" Charles teased, dodging a jab from Prescott.

"The plot thickens!" Alex teased in turn.

The dinner party was animated with jesting and coy remarks. When Alex met Sarah's gaze, however, she felt her face grow warm, as if she were cozying up to a fireplace in the winter. *Could this be love?* she wondered. She had seen that her mother and father had remained in love all these years, and she wondered if her feeling was one that would endure the tests of time as well. "My intentions are for marriage," Alex had said. A shiver of excitement coursed through her as she forced herself again to pay attention to the discussion at hand.

"Dr. Wright, how do you feel about this wondrous occasion?" Alex inquired.

Our marriage, could that be what he is talking about? No, it must be the war again, Sarah thought disappointedly.

"As you know, I was born and raised here in Virginia. I am loyal to the soil that has prospered me and kept my family in peace. But now I must confess that a peaceful settlement had been my hope and secession the choice I feared. I believe a war will result that will destroy far more than it maintains." Dr. Wright had beads of perspiration on his brow as he spoke.

"Forgive me for saying so, sir, but your fearful perception of current events could be conceived by some as a lack of patriotism rather than idealism. I fear not the outcome of this war, but rather your standing in this community should you speak openly of your concerns. Perhaps, if you saw some of our brilliant military men in action, as I do, your fears would be put to rest," Alex offered graciously.

"Perhaps," Dr. Wright replied.

As the conversation droned on about the prospects of war and its various consequences, Sarah considered her escape.

"If you gentlemen will excuse me, I'm going to the garden for some fresh air," Sarah said, hoping Alex would volunteer to join her.

"I will be outside momentarily to join you, Sarah," Alex said distractedly.

Charles and Prescott elbowed each other making kissing noises until a steely look from Mrs. Wright at the other end of the table forced them to stop.

"Brothers!" Exasperated and embarrassed, Sarah hurried from the dining room. Upon opening the back door, she was greeted by the scent of honeysuckle and the glow of the setting sun. She walked the brick path to her mother's garden. Mother sought to duplicate many of the features of a fine English manor, the formal garden being her favorite. Rows of neatly trimmed English boxwood and symmetrical plantings were pleasing to the eyes. Sarah reached her favorite spot in the garden and breathed deeply. Wisteria, just starting to bloom, stretched across a trellis that graced a marble cherub fountain.

"The smell is so wonderful one almost hates for summer to arrive and the wisteria to leave," Alex said in a sultry tone.

Startled, Sarah dropped the blossom she had just picked.

"I...I...didn't hear you coming," Sarah stammered.

"I didn't mean to frighten you, my love." Stepping nearer, he sat her down on a bench. Whispering into her ear he said, "Make me the happiest man in Virginia and marry me, Sarah Elizabeth Wright." Alex caressed her shaking hand as he placed his grandmother's ring on her finger. This was his promise of marriage, and his safe return from war.

Sarah smiled at Alex and blinked back tears of happiness and fear as they embraced. She had known this moment would come one day, but she felt so young, and Alex was such a fine, young gentleman just starting a brilliant military career.

"It is a beautiful ring, Alex. Yes, I would be honored to be your wife." Sarah was warm, dizzy and giddy all at once.

"We will have to wait until this war is over. I don't want my new bride to be alone at home without me."

"I know. I can wait..." Sarah started to speak, but Alex interrupted with a tender kiss on her mouth.

"I can wait for you," Sarah finished. Her voice quivered strangely.

As they walked hand in hand on the criss-crossing paths of Mother's garden, Sarah wondered how long the wait might be.

CHAPTER 3

"Will you be joining us in the sewing circle this afternoon, Sarah?" Mrs. Wright barely looked up from her furious knitting of woolen socks as she spoke.

"Yes, ma'am. Whatever I can do for the Cause." Sarah considered the changes the past year had brought with the Cause. In a barely audible voice she marvelled, "It's odd. We used to have parties just for fun. The only ones we have now are to sew shirts for soldiers or weave cloth. Strange times."

Gone were the dances with all the eligible young men and ladies of the surrounding countryside attending. The few boys and men who remained were either very young, very old, or sick. Papa was relieved, although somewhat ashamed, he wouldn't have to fight since his medical services were more vital to the incoming wounded from local battles.

Wounded. Alex. It had been weeks since she had heard any news. Sarah absentmindedly played with the gold ring on her finger. *Could he continue to escape harm?* she wondered.

"Mother, I will be out back with Papa," Sarah said quickly, ready to dodge the inevitable fire.

"Indeed, Sarah, your manners. Ladies don't enjoy sickness and death...if it weren't for the War, I would absolutely forbid it." Mother must have realized the uselessness of continuing as she stared out the window.

Sarah noticed her mother's simple cotton clothes. They weren't as fresh and stylish as before the war, since she shared more of the burden of running the farm. Only the house servants remained because most of the field servants were impressed by the Confederates to help dig trenches.

What concerned Sarah the most was not the material changes, but the emotional ones. Lines etched on Mother's face revealed her concern for her six children. Thomas, two years Sarah's senior, was at the moment defending the capitol, so close to home yet worlds apart. Young thirteen-year-old Prescott did his best in the Home Guard, determined not to let his age keep him neither from action, nor from impressing Victoria. Charles, only eleven, preferred to stay home and keep Julia and Carter, the two youngest, company. Mother's biggest concern was probably Sarah. She scurried around her father's medical office tending to the sick as if she hadn't been raised to be a lady. Not that Mother didn't support the Cause, but Sarah seemed to enjoy herself. Mother looked at Sarah's gentle blond curls surrounding her fair, round face and wondered how she had failed in her upbringing. A delightful, gentle girl Sarah doubtlessly was. But her preferred past time was a concern to a woman like Elizabeth Louise, who was brought up in a proper Richmond home.

The bright fuschia blossoms contrasted with the glossy green foliage, making springtime even lovelier on the farm. Inhaling whiffs of azaleas peeking around the corner of the building, Sarah entered the small office.

All four windows of the office had their curtains pulled back to let in as much light as possible. In the center of the room, a small, long wooden table about waist high served as the examining table. A pitcher and basin stand next to it reminded Sarah of Papa's passion for cleanliness. Books filled the shelves on the wall across from the door. A desk piled high with papers and medical volumes stood near the bookshelves. Across from the desk stood a cabinet with assorted glass bottles of medicine and dried herbs. Bandages and cotton sat ready for the next patient.

It is very humble compared to what Chimborazo Hospital in Richmond is supposed to have, Sarah thought, *8,000 beds, five soup kitchens, and a bakery that produces 10,000 loaves of bread each day.*

Papa sat at the desk, his head in his hands, as Sarah gently put her hands on his shoulders. "How is the Newton boy?" Sarah asked, remembering the young boy's face as he lie there, delirious with fever. The sick seemed to come in more frequently now.

"Much improved. You did a fine job with him, Sarah. You were right in administering the laudanum and peppermint. You are a splendid nurse, my dear." Papa smiled, but his eyes were sad. "Did you hear the good news?" He opened the telegram when Sarah indicated she hadn't. "Corporal Brooke alive-stop-hopes to arrive at Wright home soon-stop," he read.

Sarah flushed at the thought of Alex. *Would we still wait until this war is over, or is he on his way home to marry me? No, how selfish. Surely he has so many responsibilities right now. How long will the war go on?*

"What is this war really about?" Sarah surprised herself by entering the male world of conversation with such a daring political question. Yet she knew of Papa's apathy to the war, though he tried to be discreet for his family's protection. More than one house had been searched under the suspicion of its occupants being Union spies. Sarah remembered finding, not long ago, a brown and tattered copy of *Uncle Tom's Cabin* in this office. It was obviously read and pondered over many times. Sarah read it herself, and felt too many stereotypes were used. Yet, Dr. Wright was dedicated to Virginia, to a life he loved and embraced for his family. He seemed trapped, like so many, in an economic system that appeared to work but was destined to fail because it was based on forced servitude of a large part of its population.

After a long pause and a few puffs on his pipe, Dr. Wright replied, "Sarah Elizabeth, you do surprise me at times with your impertinence. But I know you are no silly girl filled with foolish notions. You see the inherent wrong in our way of life, yet it's not so easily remedied. We personally are not like some in their treatment of our servants, but I don't believe God looks down in approval. Not a word, my dear, to any, or they'll have my head for treason, deserter of the noble Cause. I do not agree with the Northern government intruding on our soil, taking away the states' individual rights. That is where I take my stand for our wonderful land, our precious Virginia. Do you see, my dear?" Papa said, pleading forgiveness with his eyes. "Your Alex doesn't share my views. You will marry soon, he will be your authority, and you must abide by his judgment." Then, after clearing his throat, he said, "See if Mother needs any help preparing for

Cousin Felicity's visit. I'm sure her parents will be relieved to get her out of Richmond. These are such uncertain times."

Yes, uncertain times, Sarah thought. *Richmond is in danger as the capitol of the Confederacy. Having Felicity come and stay indefinitely will be a pleasant change in mundane times.*

Rain gently tapped on the roof and windows. A smoky gray sky hung overhead as Sarah rocked gently in the shelter of the covered front porch awaiting Felicity's arrival. A tired looking horse pulling a rough coach passed through the gate. The driver pulled up to the plank walk-way leading to the front porch, a remnant of when the house was once a hotel. Hopping down, he opened the coach door for his passenger. Felicity stepped down the two steps, her midnight blue dress looked fresh despite the journey from the city. Her auburn hair was fixed in an upsweep, but stray curls fell around her neck. Her green eyes glistened when she saw Sarah on the porch.

"Come greet your cousin in this dreadful rain!" Felicity called cheerfully, attempting to shelter herself with a dainty parasol.

Sarah ran down the steps and embraced her cousin, disregarding the rain that now fell in smaller, wind-swept drops. "It is so wonderful to have you here. I hope all is well with Aunt Maria and Uncle Thomas. Was the trip tiresome?"

"Whoa, Sarah, one question at a time," Felicity said with a laugh. "Yes, all is well with Mama and Papa. Richmond is becoming more frightening than ever, Sarah. Soldiers patrol the streets, fights break out regularly as fears and tensions wear on everyone. Mama thought I'd be safer out here in the country for a while." With a quick glance and nod toward Peachy to be of help, giddy with laughter, Sarah and Felicity ascended the front steps. A slender black girl loaded down with a heavy burden trailed behind.

The house smelled of magnolia blossoms that Sarah had clipped off of the towering tree behind the house. Its lemony fragrance helped disguise the musty smell that seemed to hang in the air. The wide pine floor boards shined from the efforts of Peachy and Mary. A red velvet settee and mahogany tables lined the wide hallway that was used often as a second parlor.

At the far end of the hall, Felicity stood looking out the back door at a small, white frame building near the house. "Dr. George Washington Wright" was carefully painted on the door. A worn looking elderly man rested on the rough bench beside the door, waiting his turn with the doctor, despite the rain.

"Sarah, your father still works out of that old lean-to, mmm? It seems he could have something finer. Mama says if he would have stayed in Richmond, he'd be a partner in a fine practice right now."

"I imagine Papa has done what he wishes. It is not my place to judge," Sarah said in defence of her father. As soon as she spoke she thought, *Of course, this practice does not always provide enough income for our family to live on when patients don't pay, but our tobacco crops and apple orchard help out.* "Since the field hands are occasionally busy digging trenches for the army, the house servants and we children maintain the kitchen garden," Sarah offered as the explanation to the rather meager looking patch beside the house. "In fact, Julia has grown quite fond of her lettuce plants."

"My word. Your hands must be in an awful state with that sort of labor. I'm afraid I won't be able to help. My hands may not be able to play the piano nearly as well with calloused fingers," Felicity said matter-of-factly.

"As you wish, you are our guest," Sarah offered politely.

⌛ ⌛ ⌛

The dinner table was alive with bubbly laughter from the girls as they recounted cherished memories of times together.

"Sarah, remember the time both of you put on a fashion show? You two were the most precious little ladies. Then you entertained us; Felicity on the piano and Sarah with her poetry," Mother said. Her eyes were a bit misty.

"Yes, I was playing 'Le Retour de Printemps' while Sarah was passionately reading her poem about Springtime. How did that verse go, Sarah?" Felicity asked sheepishly.

"Oh, it was nothing, really, I..." Sarah stammered.

"Rebirth, reawakening,

Vitality unguarded

Reaching, ever reaching

Until beautiful life is restored..."

The familiar voice came from the doorway. Everyone gasped as Alex walked in with a slight limp. His uniform looked worn but still dignified.

"My, oh, my what a surprise!" Mrs. Wright was the only one able to find her tongue.

"Yes, Alex, I, we didn't expect you." Sarah blurted out. "But, a pleasant surprise it is, of course!" Sarah stood and kissed Alex's inclined cheek.

"Well, now that is more like the greeting I had hoped for!" Alex laughed. "I decided to take a mini-ball in the foot so that I'd have a reason to leave for a day or two."

Met with exclamations of care and pity, Alex bathed in the concern, all the while staring at his beloved Sarah.

"Have we won yet?" Charles questioned. His question, although not considered impossible, was still met with a chorus of laughter from the others.

"Not yet, Charles. General Lee still is faithfully leading us on the glorious path to victory," Alex said.

"Is your cavalry unit near here?" Dr. Wright asked.

"For a short while, sir. I am only to spend the evening here, and then I am expected back at camp."

Peachy followed Mary into the basement, her face bewildered. "What is it? Cat got your tongue?" Mary asked.

"She loves him."

"Yes, that Miss Sarah shore do put store by that fellow, an' a handsome one at that he is..."

"No'm. Miss Felicity, she looked at him with her heart."

CHAPTER 4

The cold ripped through Sarah as she and Peachy walked back to the house from feeding the horses. With Dr. Wright busier than ever taking care of the sick and wounded, and Thomas defending the city, Sarah took on more of the responsibilities in managing the household. "Mother just seems to have entered a condition," Papa would say when Sarah questioned her mother's behavior.

"Poor Prescott and Charles," Sarah said as she walked, noticing that the fall chill had humbly given way to the hard winter cold. "Mama can barely take care of Julia and Carter it seems. If it weren't for practicing maneuvers with the Home Guard, Prescott would be off getting into trouble, no doubt. And Charles seems to live in a world of make believe without a war." She felt a pang of envy for her younger brother who could forget, if only for a time, the misery that sometimes engulfed her.

Sarah focused hard on Peachy as she walked beside her. Peachy's fair, amber skin was the product of a white grandfather and his slave. Peachy had grown up alongside Sarah; they were almost sisters. But, after all, Peachy was a servant, Sarah would often remind herself. Sarah marvelled at Peachy's tidiness. The pale blue scarf wound around her head framed her delicate, peaceful face. Sarah's carefully mended dress from two summers ago managed to look crisp on her graceful frame. The ivory shawl Mary had knit was snug around her shoulders.

"What ya thinking, Miss Sarah?" Peachy spoke for the first time since they had left the stables.

"How I don't know what I would do without you."

"Miss Sarah, you are very kind. Jesus has been good giving me to a kind lady like yoself. Gonna be a hard winter, I think."

"Mmm." Sarah kicked a rock in the path, sending it sailing into the woods. "I wish Alex didn't have to return to the fight."

"I don' suppose too many men wish they be fighting again. Though I think your Alex likes it right good."

"How so, Peachy."

"It's that glimmer he gets in his eye when he speaks of fighting and war and victory and the like. It's just what I think, no disrespect intended."

"Quite alright." Sarah's face looked slightly puzzled as she considered what had been said.

Once inside, the sweet smell of burning wood in the fireplaces filled the air. Sarah breathed deeply as she stood before the fire, her back to the flames. Mother sat quietly in the heavy velvet crimson chair with mahogany legs and arms that matched her favorite table. She barely looked up from her mending as she said, "Sarah, darling, you'll burn your skirts standing so close to the flames."

"Yes'm," Sarah acknowledged her mother's concern, yet remained where she stood. "Mr. Walker looked mighty fine this morning, Mother. Although, his coat needed a good combing. Such a fine stallion. I'm so glad the government hasn't 'borrowed' him like so many of our neighbor's horses. Why, you should have heard the excitement when I took him out to stretch his legs. I thought the entire barnful of beasts was going to attack in a jealous rage. They need more exercise, most definitely. Mr. Walker flew like a bird through the field. He hardly took notice of my being there. I must confess I did ride astride, the side saddle is such a nuisance..." Sarah stopped rambling on when she noticed her mother had not been listening. Her mother's sadness had become a great concern, it engulfed her, choked her like...smoke! Sarah jumped from the hearth with a screech as flames lit up her skirts!

"Sarah!" Mrs. Wright cried, rising from her chair.

"Miss Sarah, fall down!" Peachy commanded from the doorway. In a second she was beside Sarah and had rolled over her, snuffing out the small but harmful flames. Peachy stood up, her chest heaved with each breath, and she held out a steady hand to Sarah. Sarah grabbed the strong hand and stood, choking out the words, "Thank you."

Peachy grinned and turned toward the kitchen, muttering to herself but loud enough for Sarah to hear as she walked, "Don't be standin' so close next time, Miss Sarah. Nearly scared us to death."

The smell of burnt cotton and linen material filled the room. Sarah looked at her mother, who had risen from her seat and still held the worn, blue blanket she was mending. She had intended to beat out the flames with it. Sarah saw the fright in her mother's eyes and couldn't help laughing. Finally, Mrs. Wright gave way to the humor of the situation. Both women were collapsed on chairs, laughing hysterically, when Felicity walked in.

"My, it is hard to sleep with all this commotion down here. I do believe you ladies have lost your senses. What is so terribly funny? Come now, I'm in suspense!" Felicity pleaded for an explanation as she spied the burnt fabric of Sarah's skirt.

"I was on fire... Peachy, rolled... top of me. Mama... the blanket, my skirts..." Sarah attempted answers while in a fit of laughter.

"Truly, ya'll have gone mad," Felicity said as she examined Sarah's singed skirts. The deep blue fabric helped to camouflage the black framed hole in the rear of the dress.

"I must go tell Mary what a brave daughter she has," Sarah said, excusing herself.

"Sarah, before you go, I must thank you. That was the first laugh I have had in weeks. But next time, let's try not to involve fire in the humor." Mrs. Wright smiled as she hugged her eldest daughter.

Sarah felt the warm glow of love surround her as she made her way down to the basement. She stopped short on the stairs when she overheard excited voices, then slowly moved closer so she could see who was talking.

"FREE! We's free now Mary. Missuh Lincoln he's said we's free!" Peter said, pausing on each word as he grabbed Mary by the arm, animating his dark shadow on the rough brick wall.

"Yes, Peter, but I's been free all along, in here," Mary said just above a whisper, poking her long finger at her chest.

"Well, I dun care if they is good massuhs. We's people, not animals. Ain't no one gonna own me or my chilluns. We's free. Missuh Abe, he says so. And listen, Mary, 'fore long we's all goin' to meet Moses," Peter's voice was quiet but firm as he stomped his worn boots on the dirt floor.

"Well, is President Lincoln hisself gonna come down an' take us to freedom?" Mary said sarcastically.

Sarah didn't quite understand what was said, but she was pretty sure he wasn't speaking of meeting Moses in heaven. Quietly, Sarah slipped back into the hallway.

The frigid, cloudy afternoon was overcome by the dark sky of night. The crackle of fires in each room accented the quiet talk. Prescott and Felicity played chess in the drawing room while Julia, Carter and Charles played with alphabet blocks on the floor.

War seemed to affect every being, every creature, even nature itself. *Will we ever know the joy and freedoms we once embraced?* Sarah wondered as she stared out the back door window.

"Miss Sarah," Peachy whispered. Her voice was barely audible but Sarah sensed the urgency in her tone.

Peachy jerked her head toward the empty dining room and entered, but not before glancing all around. "Trouble, Miss Sarah. Some of the servants are talking about runnin'. But they plan on hurtin' some of your family first, some of the mean ones keep saying. It's not looking too good for you white folks. D'army shoulda jes kept these trouble makers. They'd kill me if they found out I opened my mouth, but Miss Sarah, you need to do something. I's scared for both our families..." Peachy's eyes watered as she spoke, but she looked just as angry as scared.

"Oh, Sweet Jesus! Help us now, Lord. What shall we do? Surely if they try to escape, the Home Guard, or even worse, the army, will spot them and hang them. Oh, how terrible. We can't let this happen. And what do they mean, hurt us? No one will hurt my family as long as I have breath." Sarah's eyes were wide and her speech quickened to meet the rapid beating of her heart.

"Now, Miss Sarah, they ain't said for certain, but I gather nothing too pretty. I told Mama ain't nobody touching the Wrights, and she said I's not big enough to stop justice being done."

"Justice! That isn't justice. We need to find out when, and how, and who.... Don't let on that you're upset, Peachy. Just go along with the plans. I'll think of something to keep our people from senseless killing." Sarah paused and stared hard at Peachy. "Why didn't you try for your freedom too?"

"I never saw sense in punishin' those who eat a bad tasting pie. It ain't their fault they are ignorant. It's the people who made the pie, it's their fault. Sides. You treat me different than most anyone. You're a friend." Peachy blushed as she clasped Sarah's hands. She had spoken the words that were in Sarah's heart all along.

"Yes, your friend. Now, there is work to be done."

Sarah stood with her face pressed against the glass, trying to distinguish Peachy's figure in the darkness as she walked towards her quarters. It was difficult to see if the slowly moving figure slightly hunched over in sadness was male or female. It was impossible to tell if the person was black or white.

"Amazing how her skin blends right into the night sky." Felicity's voice dripping sarcasm came from the doorway of the dining room.

Sarah whirled around and noticed Felicity's feline appearance, as if she were about to pounce on her prey. She had never seen Felicity like this, and it was frightening.

"Judging by what I overheard between you and your, er, friend, would I be safe to say you could be considered an abolitionist? I'm sure Alex would be so pleased to know that while he is risking his life, a very handsome life, to save this Confederate nation, you are breaking all the rules of our nation. What an honor it will be for him to have a darkie-lover on his arm," Felicity said cooly.

"Felicity, I never...I was merely letting a faithful servant know I appreciate her." Sarah felt herself making excuses.

"Sounds like you have been keeping company with Mr. Lincoln himself, my dear. Papa always said your daddy would lead you into his anti-Southern thinking..."

"My father is anything but anti-Southern!" Sarah cut in. "He loves the South, our way of life, the state's rights. But Papa also loves people, and he believes in treating all men with respect in the sight of God." Sarah defended her father the best she knew how.

"I've always loved you, Sarah. I've admired your strength of conviction. I believe you are out of place on this one," Felicity said before she turned and walked up the stairs.

I wonder exactly what she heard, Sarah wondered, as she watched Felicity float gracefully upstairs.

CHAPTER 5

"Miss Sarah," Peachy whispered in Sarah's ear so she wouldn't wake sleeping Julia. "I need to talk to you."

Sarah sat up. Not only was it uncommon for Peachy to be in her room at night, but her sense of urgency demanded Sarah's attention.

"Isaac, from Mr. Smith's farm, told me today that the servants at Prichertts plan on joining the slaves here in two days, Saturday. There will be so many, Sarah, you can't stop them! I'm scared, for me and Mammy and Pappy and you. Isaac says a Union lady in Richmond has agreed to help all the Negroes escape."

"Union lady..." Sarah muttered, trying to remember the name of the lady who bore such a title in Felicity's neighborhood. "Do you know her name?"

"Miss Sarah, he didn't give any names. I'm sure you wouldn't know this sort of woman. If'n you did, it shore would be a danger for you and your family."

"It's alright, Peachy. I have a plan. Besides, if the rain keeps up, the creeks will keep swelling, making a hard crossing through the swamps, which is their likely route. That should discourage them. Maybe they'll abandon their plan, at least temporarily. It'll be just like Gabrielle Prosser's insurrection. Peachy, go along with the plans, but do not leave the property or I cannot guarantee your safety," Sarah gained confidence as she spoke. *Should I tell Father? Would that put Peachy at risk?*

⏳ ⏳ ⏳

Saturday morning greeted a sober Sarah with an ethereal mist blanketing the fields. Trees were shrouded by the fog. One dark tree poked a limb out of the fog, as if pointing the way to a wandering soul.

"Good morning, Felicity," Sarah said with a smile as she sat down for breakfast. "I have the most wonderful surprise. I've asked Prescott and the Home Guard to come and practice maneuvers here today. The neighboring women and girls are all invited to make it a patriotic display. What do you think? It will give us something to do other than sit and sew." Sarah munched on a warm biscuit.

"That sounds like a fine idea, Sarah," Felicity said with a slightly puzzled yet satisfied look on her face. "Perhaps I was too harsh on you the other day." She gingerly drank her coffee. "Real coffee would be so wonderful this morning, don't you agree? This nut blend is enough to make one ill."

"Sarah, Prescott says you invited this massive crowd onto our lawn. Why didn't you consult me?" Dr. Wright spoke as he entered the dining room.

"I thought it would be a wonderful surprise. It's so seldom we get surprises these days."

"Pleasant ones, anyway," Mrs. Wright said. "Let's breakfast on the front porch so we won't miss the best part. Prescott says they will have a marksmanship contest."

The house was abuzz with excitement as they settled on the porch. The fog was lifting. Sarah noticed Peachy and Mary solemnly setting the table. Peter was in the yard directing horses and drivers as they entered the yard. The older men and young boys who made up the Guard were an interesting contrast; those who had just begun to live among those full of experience. The Allen Station Guard, as they called themselves, were a rather serious group who made regular rounds in the area.

"Miss Sarah, I think you have succeeded," Peachy whispered as she served her plate.

"Let's hope this is as intense as the morning gets."

Gunshots punctuated Sarah's last words. All eyes turned towards a man on horseback galloping toward them.

"Attention, Troops! Armed Negroes on foot approaching from the west. I spied them criss-crossing through the fields near the Sheppard farm. Let's go!"

A mad scramble ensued, followed by hoops and hollers from the young ones. Sarah could see Peachy shaking, and Mary and Peter talking nervously in the yard.

"My, my what a commotion. Let's go inside, children, and let the men settle this...this...situation." Mrs. Wright looked rather pale as she ushered her flock into the house.

"Are you still in agreement of treating Negroes with respect, Sarah?" Felicity said immediately as she entered the house.

Without a word, Sarah went out the back door and into Dr. Wright's office. She began making preparations for possible injuries to bide her time while the men settled the "situation." *Perhaps I have erred in not saying something to Papa,* Sarah thought. *After all, it wouldn't have gotten this far had the men known. But Peachy's life may not have been spared by her own people had they discovered her confiding in me,* Sarah continued to play out her actions in her mind. The sound of horses pounding up the driveway brought her from her thoughts.

"Sarah, clean rags and water, quick! We must stop the bleeding!" Dr. Wright ordered as he hurried in the office carrying a wounded boy. "Prescott!" Sarah exclaimed. She could see he had been slashed with a knife in the thigh. Blood oozed from the cut, soaking his torn pants.

"Now, Sarah!" Dr. Wright shook Sarah from her shock.

Dr. Wright and Sarah worked quickly, cleaning and bandaging the wound, lest infection set in.

"Rusty knife, from the looks of it. That Negra was mighty fearless, lunging for us like he did. But you were a real soldier, Prescott. If it weren't for your quick head, he'd probably have done much worse." Dr. Wright was trying to keep a sluggish looking Prescott conscious.

"Did you catch all of them, Papa?" Sarah asked anxiously.

"All but the one who did this. One of Prichertt's, I think. And the rest are all in prison waiting their punishment, except for the one who shot himself to escape his likely hanging," Papa said solemnly. "It could have been far worse, only one injury, had the Home Guard not been so conveniently located." Dr. Wright turned to face his daughter. "You seem to have an amazing sense of timing, my dear," he added.

"God has been good to us, today," Sarah replied, avoiding eye contact with her father.

"Yes, indeed he has," Dr. Wright said, cleaning up a now sleeping Prescott. "He'll be fine, now. I think this soldier has had enough excitement for one day." With that, he carefully carried Prescott back into the house where he could rest peacefully.

Sarah continued cleaning up the office, and jumped when she heard her mother shriek at the sight of Prescott. "I better get some smelling salts, she's probably fainted," Sarah said aloud. As she turned, she caught sight of Felicity staring into the window. Her face looked unfriendly at first, until Sarah's eyes caught and held her glance.

"Well done, Cousin. Your talents are remarkable," Felicity said icily before returning to the house ahead of Sarah.

"This is precisely why Prescott doesn't need to be in the Home Guard. It is far too dangerous." Mrs. Wright was ashen with worry.

"There are boys younger than he is fighting with the men in the regular army now, Elizabeth. Prescott wants to help like his brother, Thomas. At least this way Prescott is living here at home and not in some camp, eating God knows what to stay alive and fearing for his life every minute. Be thankful, Elizabeth, he hasn't run off and joined on his own. He's a good boy, and he's fighting admirably for Virginia," Dr. Wright defended his son.

"Yes, I suppose you are right. I think I shall surely wither with worry over my boys."

"God says to cast all of your care upon Him, Elizabeth. He doesn't want you carrying this burden around."

"I love you, George."

Feeling like she was intruding on a private moment between her parents, Sarah crept upstairs to her room.

CHAPTER 6

"Sarah, may I see you in my office, please?" Dr. Wright called, as Sarah walked past the door.

"Yes, sir. What is it?" Sarah walked in and looked at the bare shelves that once were full of medical supplies.

"I need to send you to Richmond with Josiah for supplies. I would go myself, but I am needed elsewhere today. It appears a fight nearby has put quite a strain on the army surgeon, and they've asked for my help. I may be gone for several days, and I really need to restock here. I fear we may need all the supplies we can get, soon. You are familiar with what I use. I'm trusting you to get at least the most important items on this list. Is that agreeable with you?"

Sarah nodded as she took the list and read through it. "I will leave first thing. Shall I also arrange to purchase flour and such for the kitchen?"

"At about $80 a bag I don't think we'll be purchasing many. But, check with your mother to see what is needed. I must be leaving soon. Take this money, and Sarah, be careful." Dr. Wright looked deeply into his daughter's eyes and then drew her to him. He kissed her on the forehead then he left.

Sarah noted the calendar on the wall, April 7, 1863. *Two years of war. Two years robbed from us,* she thought.

Brook Avenue didn't look considerably different as the carriage made its way south to Richmond. Children still ran and played hide and seek, and spilled their laughter over the adult anguish that surrounded them. Crops still grew, although meager some of them were. Spring flowers were blooming, and Dogwood trees were sharing their pink and white flowers with passers by.

But, the Wright household, along with most of the South, was feeling squeezed. Northern blockades were working and forcing the Confederate Government to turn to its people for their horses, then food and extra clothing to supply the fighting forces.

"Miss Sarah, ma'am, where shall I go first?" Josiah asked as they approached Broad Street.

"Let's take care of business on Main Street," Sarah said, watching passersby hurrying along.

Driving south on Ninth Street, Sarah admired the capitol building. The tall, white pillars on the front porch made it resemble the Maison Carree in Nimes, France. Sarah remembered an engraving of the ancient temple and knew Jefferson modeled their own capitol after it. She suddenly felt proud that Virginia had such a beautiful building designed by the Father of Democracy.

How lovely it all looks, Sarah thought, looking at the green, well-manicured, sloping lawn that skirted the Capitol.

At Main Street, Josiah stopped the carriage and helped Sarah down. "I'll be right along with you, ma'am. Just let me park this here horse."

"I'll be fine, Josiah. Why don't you see to a new shoe for Mr. Walker. I will meet you back here in two hours." Sarah walked off toward Eleventh Street, leaving Josiah to mumble, "I don't think Dr. Wright is gunna like you traipsin' around town, but I reckon you is a big girl."

"Justice! Fair prices for all!"

Sarah heard shouting as she neared the corner of Eleventh. "What on earth is that all about?" Sarah wondered aloud as a mob of yelling, hysterical women approached her. Wild eyes and tattered clothes seemed to be the uniform of these desperate looking women. They moved forward to the storefronts.

"No more inflation! The Yankees won't kill us, starvation will!" Some yelled as they smashed into bakeries and butcher shops, carrying away bread, hams and salted herring. One woman tried dragging a bag of flour with her, but it was torn open on the cobblestones, and spilled it's precious contents to be trodden underfoot. Ripping, tearing and grabbing whatever they could, the women made their way north on Eleventh Street toward Sarah.

Sarah was dumbfounded by the confusion and allowed the crowd to carry her along with them. "To the Capitol!" was the frenzied cry. Sarah felt their heavy breathing and their warm perspiration as they pushed and shoved toward their destination. She felt their frustration as she glanced at the angry faces near her. Tired, hungry-looking women driven to action surrounded her. It was impossible for Sarah to break free until they reached the capitol grounds.

With the once peaceful lawn underfoot, the crowd thinned out, and Sarah was loose of her prison. But the crowds shouting didn't cease until President Davis appeared. He began throwing money out of his pockets, begging the women to blame the Yankees, not the Southern Government. He was clearly sorry for their frustration but powerless to do anything more.

"How I pity that man...the burden he carries," Sarah said to no one in particular.

"Don't pity him, Missy, nor the likes of him. This has been a rich man's war and a poor man's fight from the beginnin'," an acid-tongued, heavy-set woman said with contempt.

The crowd was not satisfied. No one was leaving. Their grumblings and threats increased, and they ignored the demands to disperse. Finally, President Davis ordered soldiers to start firing into the crowd. Women went running in a hurry.

Lord, let me out of here alive, Sarah entreated God, as she frantically made her way back to where she was to meet Josiah.

⌛ ⌛ ⌛

It wasn't until they had started to leave Richmond with the packages secured in the carriage, that Sarah revealed her eventful afternoon to Josiah.

"I shore is glad you ain't been hurt, Miss Sarah, or Dr. Wright would have me whipped, he would."

"Oh, Josiah, Papa has never whipped any of the servants. He wouldn't start now, either." Sarah sighed, feeling relief the day's episode was over.

"No'm, he ain't never done harm to any of us. But jes' the same, I wouldn't want to face him if'n his angel was hurt in my care," Josiah said thoughtfully.

Sarah heard faint, distant rumbles as they approached the Wright home at dusk.

"Either fightin' or thunder. Can't tell the difference no more. Seems like it's one or the other every day now," Josiah said.

"Uh huh," Sarah said, searching the sky for signs of either as she alighted from the carriage.

"Sarah, come quickly! There is a young soldier here with a bullet wound, and Papa isn't home, and no one else knows what to do. Mr. Smith sent him over this way hoping Papa would be here. Do you know what to do?"

Jumping from the wagon, Sarah trailed after Charles who was already heading toward Dr. Wright's office. "It's Ashton Taylor, Sarah. He ran off to the fighting. He wasn't even enlisted, but he thought he could help. Before he even made it to the battle, a Union picket shot him in the leg. He rode home as fast as he could. Please help him, Sarah," Charles begged as he lit the lantern. Darkness was now upon them.

"I'll do what I can, Charles," Sarah said, gazing at Charles' friend, laying on the table in the center of the room. Ripping his pants off below his left knee, Sarah washed the wound and checked the depth of the mini-ball.

"You are awfully brave, Ashton. This must have really hurt, and I haven't heard boo from you," Sarah comforted the ten-year-old boy. *Dear God, children are fighting the war adults have started,* Sarah thought as she prepared the knife and lantern. "Hold the light here, Charles, so I can see."

"Yes'm." Charles spoke quietly, his eyes still glued to Ashton's leg.

Sarah felt eyes fixed upon her. Glancing up, she saw Felicity peering in through the door. Her deep green dress revealed her lovely figure and highlighted her green eyes. Ashton managed to look embarrassed when he looked up at her. Sarah was less worried when she saw that Ashton was still coherent enough to notice her cousin's beauty.

"Do you need any help, Sarah?" Felicity asked softly as she entered the office.

"I could use another lantern on the other side of the table, more clean towels, and a fresh basin of water." Sarah closed her eyes as she focused on how she needed to remove the bullet without damaging the leg.

"You can do it, Sarah, I know you can," Charles whispered.

With a brief smile, Sarah proceeded to remove the mini-ball successfully. Ashton, who had given way to the precious bit of chloroform that was put to his nose, would be on his way to recovery. Charles smiled, gave Sarah an awkward pat on the back, then ran to tell Mother that all was well while Sarah bandaged Ashton.

Tired, filthy, ragged, but feeling a great sense of accomplishment, Sarah finally retired to the house.

CHAPTER 7

The train's whistle was sharp as it approached Allen's Station, not even a half-mile from the Wright's home. Dr. Wright and his neighbors had depended on its regularity in transporting goods to and from Richmond. A nine-mile journey by train wasn't a bad trip, although Dr. Wright clearly preferred that his family travel by coach or horseback rather than the "iron horse."

I wonder who or what it will bring this time, Sarah thought, gazing west toward the tracks. She had loved to go to sleep with the rhythmic rumble of the train in the night. Lately, though, the distant rumble of cannons seemed more prevalent.

Even though the November chill had settled in, Sarah still preferred to sit outside on the porch when she needed to think or just be alone. Carefully unfolding a letter from her brother Thomas, Sarah reread his words with tenderness.

June 30, 1863

Dear Mother and Father and family,

I have been away these last two and half years fighting for our Confederate nation. It is with great honor I have defended both the citizens of our nation and the causes for which the Bonnie Blue stands, especially freedom to live as you see fit. However, it is not without disappointment and regret for the time I have been separated from my loving family and friends.

Other boys, just like me, have been living off of almost nothing. In good times we've eaten slosh, which is cornmeal and bacon grease for you civilians, and peanuts and bacon. When we ran out of coffee, we would make our own blend with potatoes or peanuts or whatever we could scrounge up. At times we have impressed rations from farmers, or killed squirrels, even dogs sometimes. It's been hard. I hope it has been worth it.

We are in Pennsylvania now. General Lee hopes to defeat the North on Northern ground. You won't receive this letter 'til well after whatever battle will soon begin. I pray it is my own hand that delivers it and not someone else in my brigade that survives me.

I would surely like to think I will be coming home soon for some of Mary's fine cooking - and to beat Prescott at chess. I pray Sarah will be a happy wife with Corporal Brooke.

Give Charles, Carter and Julia kisses and hugs for me.

I love you all and miss each one of you terribly.

Love,
Thomas

The letter had been received two months previously, two months after it was written. The death notice on the bulletin board of the *Richmond Enquirer* came first. Tears had splattered the ink of Thomas' last words.

"Somehow he knew, didn't he, Mother?" Sarah asked after reading the letter the first time. "He knew he would not make it through any more of the trials war had brought. Gettysburg would be his final resting place. He knew, didn't he?"

Did Thomas die for a reason? Was his sacrifice noticed, recognized at all? Sarah ached inside for the answers to her questions really since the start of the war.

"Sarah, I thought you might like to read this," Dr. Wright said coming through the front door. "It amazes me that we can receive copies of Northern papers, yet we can't manage to get any more food. I heard Mr. Prichertt say a bag of flour was going for $250 yesterday in Richmond. Through the roof, these prices are! They're trying to starve us out, I'm sure of it. It's not as unpleasant as bloodshed, but it's killing just the same. Anyhow, I didn't mean to disturb you, just thought you might like to see this, that's all." Dr. Wright had lowered his thundering complaint about inflation to a tender half-whisper when he noticed what Sarah had been reading. "Alex sent word through a wounded soldier, who was discharged on account he lost both legs. He says he is fine, and he hopes to sneak by here again soon." Not noticing any change in Sarah's sober demeanor, Dr. Wright left Sarah to examine the article he had proffered from his pocket.

Sarah skimmed the article from the New York paper relating the recent dedication ceremony in Gettysburg, Pennsylvania. It stated that the chief speaker was Edward Everett with comments from President Abraham Lincoln. The description given of Lincoln coincided with everything Sarah had heard about him. He was tall, awkwardly built, with a tall top hat, unattractive face and clumsy appearance. His 250 word speech lasted just under two minutes, *yet it said far more than Everett ever could,* Sarah thought as she read the words Mr. Lincoln had spoken.

"How could a man thought to be such a fool be so wise?" Sarah wondered aloud at his genius. His cause, the human cause, seemed too radical, so genuine, it frightened her. *Could he be right? Is it possible for the South to be right at the same time? Have we all been fighting each other when the evil is attitudes? Why have so many been allowed to die like Thomas?*

Sarah wept as she read the statistics of that July battle once again. Wounded piled up in nearby homes...carpets soaked with blood...Union casualties about 23,000...Confederate casualties about 28,000. *Clearly no one wins at war,* Sarah concluded.

Folding the paper under her arm, Sarah entered the house. Felicity was playing the piano, Mrs. Wright was in her chair sewing another shirt for another soldier. *Another soldier, just like Thomas, who may find an end, just like Thomas. Who has a family, just like Thomas. Who meant something alive, yet appears to be meaningless in death, just like Thomas.*

The piece Felicity played was serene, peaceful. It didn't match the hurricane inside of Sarah. Her inward battle was just as real as the battle being fought all over the North and the South robbing homes of brothers, fathers and sons.

"That was lovely, Felicity. What was the name of that piece?" Mrs. Wright asked without looking up from her sewing.

"It was 'Italian Concerto' by Bach," Felicity answered, turning from the piano to see Sarah standing near the door, absorbed in thought. "Come here, Sarah.

I've been wondering where you've been. Did you hear the good news? Our Alex is fine."

"Yes, yes I did," Sarah answered in a barely audible voice, noticing the pronoun Felicity chose.

"Sarah, are you alright?" Mrs. Wright asked, examining Sarah's disheveled appearance and disturbed look.

"I think I'm finally starting to be right," Sarah said, pulling herself up the stairs to the solace of her bed.

CHAPTER 8

The ever ascending wall of gray darkened the sky. Pale green leaves of Osage orange trees punctuated the eerie clouds. Scraggly, fungus-encrusted dead limbs raised knarled fingers upward in protest against the increasingly dark, foreboding mass. *Surely this is some storm brewing!* Sarah thought. *One can understand how the ancient people imagined gods of the sky displaying their anger.* "Thank the Lord I can trust in The God who created it all," Sarah said as she walked down the drive to where her father was talking with some elderly men from nearby farms.

"Did you hear what President Davis said in his introductory speech at the Second Confederate Congress? He accused the Federal Troops of barbarism, and rightly so. Courageous fellow, that President Davis, making such a noble speech so soon after the accident," Mr. Prichertt said.

"What accident are you referring to, Paul?" asked Mr. Calvin, a strange-looking man with a large nose.

"Why Jeff Davis' young son Joe died from a fall off the back steps of their home just a few days ago, April 30, I believe. Tragic, tragic thing for our leader," Mr. Prichertt continued, shifting his excessive weight as he talked. "Well, I heard tell this morning that General Jenkins was killed yesterday, bless his soul, and General Longstreet was wounded. The way it's sounding, I think it was by some of our own men."

"No! Couldn't be!"

"Fighting up in those woods had to be fierce. Why the way things echo off of trees, like when you're deer hunting, or hunting runaways, it's enough to spook a man for certain. And fires, Lawd, those dry leaves laying all over the ground would be a terror to fight. I heard the fires killed right many. All I know is, we better start winning some ground here, or they'll be approaching Richmond before too long." Ending his sermon with a rather purposeful stream of spit, Mr. Calvin hooked his fingers through his suspenders and rocked back and forth on his heels.

"If what your saying is true, gentlemen, we may need to consider securing our homes a bit more. Find whatever food you can spare and hide it. Your precious things too, gold watches and the like, it would be wise to secure those items." Dr. Wright didn't sound fearful but thoughtful as he spoke. "As always, I will be glad to help anyone who needs help. I'll need some help from you all as well. Any towels or linens you can spare, send them here. If there is any fighting done in our area, I need to prepare for possible wounded. Buckets, blankets, whatever may be of use to care for the injured would be appreciated. I hope I am wrong. Not dead wrong, though." Dr. Wright joined the others in an uneasy laugh.

"Is there anything I can do, Father?" Sarah asked, stepping closer to the group of men.

Surprised by her presence, Dr. Wright jumped slightly. "Why, Sarah, I didn't know you were here. Gentlemen, this lovely young lady will turn twenty on May the fifteenth." Dr. Wright encircled Sarah's thin waist with his arm.

"My, you don't say. And not a bride yet, imagine!" old Mr. Prichertt exclaimed.

"You forget, old man, she is to marry Corporal Brooke when this war is over. I swear you can be told something ten times and still claim to have never heard it at all," Mr. Calvin teased.

Noticing Sarah's embarrassment, Dr. Wright continued, "Sarah, would you mind letting your mother know these two gentlemen will be joining us for tea this afternoon."

"No, no, that's alright. None of us has food to spare. We won't impose on your kindness. Do let us know if you hear any more news," Mr. Calvin called as he and Mr. Prichertt turned to leave and were spattered by large drops of rain that were beginning to fall.

"Father, did you really mean what you said about hiding food and bringing towels and all that other? Is it coming that close to us?" Sarah's eyes were wide with fear and disbelief. When Thomas was killed, it was a far away battle. Even though she often heard the distant sounds of war, she never believed it would come to her doorstep.

"There's no telling, Sarah dear. I just think it wise to take some precautionary measures since there has been fighting all around Spotsylvania these last few days. Oh, that it would all end soon. All the suffering, all the hatred, that it would all end soon."

Sarah watched as her father made his way slowly up the drive, never looking at what was around him yet very aware of what was near.

"Four more days until your birthday, Sarah. What are you wishing for?" Felicity was playfull as Sarah came down the stairs looking like she'd had a fitful sleep.

"Well, now, I think we all know the answer to that question," Mrs. Wright answered with a smile.

"I wish for peace," Sarah said simply, trying not to alarm the delicate ladies with the information that buzzed in her head.

Sarah sat down at the piano, lightly touching the keys.

"I do believe Sarah intends to play for us!" Felicity laughed at the prospect.

"No, indeed, I was just admiring how easily the keys release sound under the slightest pressure. It's amazing."

"Mmm." Felicity looked at Mrs. Wright and shrugged her shoulders.

"I wonder if it plans on raining this entire Spring. We surely have had a fair amount of rain lately, haven't we?" Mrs. Wright spoke to no one in particular.

"Just listen to the thunder, Mama. It seems to keep coming," Charles said, pausing between bites of a biscuit.

Sarah walked to the windows and peered out at the cloudy day. Pressing her ear to the glass, she listened intently.

"That's not thunder, Charles," Sarah said with a slight quiver in her voice.

"What is it then?" The whole room inquired.

"Take a look."

Sarah moved back to let them all look at the long procession of Union cavalrymen and soldiers on foot. Row after row of blue uniforms paraded down Mountain Road. The thundering of their feet and the hooves of their horses competed against the crashing of thunderclouds overhead.

Sarah and the boys strained to see through the heavy rain. Finally, they went out on the porch for a better look.

"Come inside at once, children! We must hide for safety! What if some of those soldiers decide to stray and come here for trouble! Come inside, come inside!" Mrs. Wright pleaded frantically with her inquisitive children.

With all her chicks back in the nest, Mrs. Wright proceeded to lock all the windows and doors and usher the little ones to the third floor where they could watch in safety from the windows.

"Sarah, go get your father from his office. He surely must have heard this commotion. Where is he now, I wonder?"

Sarah could see her father, standing at the side of the house, hands on hips, watching the procession at the road.

"What does it mean, Father?" Sarah asked as she approached him.

"Battle nearby, it appears. It sounds as if they are ripping up the railroad at the crossing. They won't leave till they've done a thorough job." Dr. Wright looked weary yet peaceful, despite the sounds of destruction coming from Allen's Station.

Shouting and bugle blares erupted from the column of men. An important looking man, General from what

Sarah could tell, rode to the front of the line and talked with the leader of the procession. Some commands were shouted, and the men began to gallop eastward toward their goal.

Clinging to her father now, Sarah begged him to come in out of the rain. "You can watch from the window, Papa. You are getting soaked."

"Thomas had to endure many days in the rain, Sarah. Many a boy and man have spent their lives in the rain."

The blank stare on his face told Sarah that further pleading would be futile. Shivering as she entered the house, she hurried to the parlor fireplace to warm herself.

"Remember what I tole you 'bout standing near the fire, Miss Sarah," Peachy said from the corner of the dark room. A smile was in her voice, but Sarah knew she was afraid.

"Peachy, are you alright? I haven't seen you today, didn't know where you'd gone."

"Just waiting for the rain to end, that's all."

"Me too, Peachy, me too." Sarah walked toward Peachy and gave her a hug.

"Your Mama and the others are upstairs. The whole house is so dark I can hardly see my hand. Rainy days like this are always so dark." Peachy was nervous as she spoke. "We hid some hams up inside the cubbyhole in the kitchen fireplace. Miss Elizabeth has money hid up in her belt around her waist. No soldier better be looking there. Dr. Wright sure is smart telling us to hide stuff."

"Everything will be fine. Let's go upstairs with the others. Papa won't come in out of the rain. I've tried to talk to him; it's no use," Sarah lamented as they walked toward the stairs.

A loud pounding came at the front door. Sarah gasped when she saw that it was a small group of Union soldiers through the glass.

"Open up, in the name of the Federal Government!" they cried.

What shall I do? Sarah wondered.

"If we don't move, they probably won't see us. Maybe they'll just leave," Peachy whispered.

"No they won't. They'll knock down the door and force their way through the house, just like they've done all over the South."

Sarah walked to the door and opened it slightly. "What is it you want?" she demanded.

"Well, if it isn't a lovely little Southern princess. There is a whole lot we are wantin', but we'll settle for some food. We've got a hungry lot. Let us in for a look around." The soldier was short in stature but appeared to be the leader of the scavengers; his tone was demanding.

Standing aside while the four men entered, Sarah asked pointedly, "Why aren't you men with the rest of your army? They all seemed in an awful hurry."

With a chuckle the leader replied, "Yes, little lady, they were in a hurry, and we'll be joining them as quick as we can. There's a fair battle going on up the road a bit that we plan on winning. Now, if you'll let us back to our business..." He turned and joined the others searching for food and valuables.

"Shame we can't take some live souvenirs with us," a small, sinister looking soldier said, eyeing Sarah and Peachy.

"You all been hiding stuff, or starving. Which is it?" the leader asked Sarah quietly.

"You Yankee vermin have starved us. There is nothing for you here," Sarah answered, a bitter edge in her voice.

One of the men moved as though to slap her, but the leader backed him down with a stare. Under different circumstances Sarah would have found him very attractive. His raven hair, olive complexion and rugged face made him a handsome man.

"It is my wish we could have met under more fortunate circumstances, young lady," the leader said, ushering the other men out the door and into the rain.

Sarah turned as she closed the door and saw her father at the back of the foyer, gun in hand. "You did well, my dear. I'm sorry you and Peachy had to deal with that unpleasantness."

With a deep sigh, Sarah sank to the steps. "At least they did us no harm. They didn't take a thing. I think they really were hungry."

"War makes beggars of us all, Sarah." Dr. Wright silently moved to stand guard on the porch.

Sarah and Peachy joined the rest of the family upstairs.

"Peachy, I think the rain is just beginning," Sarah whispered, as they listened in the shadows. Cannons boomed nearby for the next few hours.

CHAPTER 9

The sounds of battle slowly diminished as Sarah, Peachy, Mrs. Wright and the children sat in the dimly lit room. Quietly, Mrs. Wright began quoting the Twenty-Third Psalm.

"The Lord is my Shepherd, I shall not want. He maketh me lie down in green pastures. He leadeth me beside the still waters. He restoreth my soul. He leadeth me in the paths of righteousness for His name's sake."

Now seven more voices joined hers in increasing strength and volume. "Yea, though I walk through the valley of the shadow of death, I will fear no evil: for Thou art with me; Thy rod and Thy staff, they comfort me. Thou preparest a table before me in the presence of mine enemies; Thou anointest my head with oil; my cup runneth over. Surely goodness and mercy shall follow me all the days of my life; and I will dwell in the house of the Lord forever." Peace filled their hearts and minds as they waited for the unknown.

Sounds of a wagon and galloping horsemen came from the road. Sarah and Charles looked out the window and saw Union cavalrymen talking to their father. Motioning to the house, the men proceeded up the drive. Dr. Wright followed with his head bowed.

Sarah saw ten men piled into the wagon; all were wounded. Several more men on horseback, who looked unfit to ride any further, made their way to the house. There appeared to be about thirty injured men in total.

The able-bodied soldiers lifted the wounded and carried them to the front door.

"What is it, Sarah?" Mrs. Wright asked, cradling sleeping Julia and Carter.

Sarah looked at Charles, whose brown eyes were wide with fright. "Wounded soldiers, Mother. It appears they will be cared for here. Father will need my help. Charles and I will go." Sarah failed to mention they were Union soldiers.

"Do be careful, Sarah. Keep an eye on Charles," Mrs. Wright whispered as she rocked the babies, and hummed softly.

Sarah left, careful not to wake the sleeping Felicity. *One can only imagine how she would react,* Sarah thought.

Sarah had never seen so many injured men at once. They occupied every available inch of floorspace in the hall. The stench of warm blood oozing from filthy wounds made her stomach turn as she moved from soldier to soldier giving the conscious ones water to drink.

Sarah gasped when she recognized the leader of the foraging group. His face was bloody, he was missing fingers, and his legs bore multiple wounds. Barely conscious, he moved his head slowly to look at Sarah with his intense green eyes.

She was nervous. She wanted to run away, yet she felt compelled to stay. "Looks like our men found a target," Sarah said smartly, still angry at his earlier intrusion.

"My luck they didn't kill me, just maim me for life." He tried to joke, but talking took too much strength, and he began coughing fiercely.

Examining his leg wounds, Sarah said, "They don't appear to be too serious. Of course, I won't be able to do more than clean up your hand...but the mini-ball wounds should be no trouble at all."

"I suppose you must be a nurse, then. You haven't even turned your head away at my horrible appearance. Like I said, it's a real shame I didn't meet you under different circumstances."

"Well, let me assure you if we had met under different circumstances, the outcome would be the same, because I'm engaged. As to your appearance, I have seen some awful things, especially lately, helping my father. He's a doctor. And I must say that you will be turning heads again soon, as soon as I stitch up that cut on your forehead." With a quick smile, Sarah proceeded to wipe off his face.

"I suppose I should ask your forgiveness for our earlier...unpleasantness. It's something I was ordered to do."

"Father says war makes beggars of us all. I'll forgive you, eventually."

"Now there's a hope I can cling to," he joked, letting out a small groan after a quick laugh.

"What is it?" Sarah asked, kneeling beside him.

"Aw, just some bruised ribs, I think, from when I fell off my horse.

"Sarah, I need you over here," Dr. Wright called, holding down a flailing young soldier. Sarah recognized him as the sinister soldier she encountered earlier. She joined her brother Charles holding him down while Dr. Wright administered some of their precious quinine to reduce his fever.

"We are prepared to pay for your supplies, sir," a slightly wounded officer said, cleaning his own wound.

"At $100 per ounce, I would hope so," Dr. Wright said, not entirely comfortable with his forced services.

Sarah returned to caring for the raven haired young soldier.

"Sarah. So that's the name you go by. I was waiting for a formal introduction, but this will do." The soldier smiled.

"And your name would be," Sarah asked officiously.

"Samuel Clay Douglas, ma'am, of the 6th New York Cavalry under Colonel Thomas C. Devin, Sheridan's First Division. And the pleasure of your acquaintance is all mine." He smiled as he feigned tipping his cap. Sarah couldn't help but smile in return.

"Apparently your vocal chords haven't been injured in the slightest, Mr. Douglas."

"Call me Sam, please. After all, you'll be cutting my body with a knife. It's only proper." Again, he mustered his grin.

After a few moments Sarah said, "There. You're all cleaned up. I'll be back in a bit after I've tended to some of these other soldiers."

"Hurry back," Sam said hoarsely as he lay his head down on the newly restained carpet.

Sarah moved from body to body, closing the lids of some when she felt no pulse.

"Who would have thought we'd be helping Yankees, of all people! Life is strange," Dr. Wright whispered to Sarah as he tended to a broken leg.

Sarah didn't feel she was being unfaithful to the Cause, because her cause was the human one. She worked so hard to spare lives; she couldn't find reasoning to consider some lives less important.

Sarah looked up the stairwell when she heard footsteps. Felicity and Mother were standing there with shock on their faces. Felicity retreated hastily up the stairs. Mother fainted where she stood. Sarah ran up the steps, cradling Mother's head in her arms. "Come on, Mama, come back. Everything will be alright. Remember our Shepherd leads us and guides us."

Mrs. Wright fluttered her lids several times before recognition set in and her hazel eyes focused on Sarah. "I'll be fine, Sarah. You go help your father now."

Sarah continued with her work, satisfied that she had her mother's blessing. Sarah worked her way back to Sam. "Charles, will you get some more water here, and another lantern, please. I need to remove the metal from his leg." Fresh blood oozed from Sam's wounds. "Hurry, he's starting to hemorrhage."

Sarah worked quickly on an unconscious Sam. Finding four mini-balls in one leg, Sarah was satisfied that she had them all. But, when she was about to stitch up the opening she had made, she noticed a fifth. "Here's one I almost missed, Sam."

"All men who are able to walk or ride, we will be departing shortly. We want to meet the others before nightfall. My apologies to the rest of you. I will be unable to wait for you to regain strength to travel. Dr. Wright assures me you will be well cared for here."

Moans rose from the few who were destined to remain behind. "No! We'll be sent to Libbey Prison for sure. Don't leave us behind!" Tears were met with silence as the officer proceeded to do what duty demanded of him. "Take us in the wagon!" the men cried.

"The wagon is gone. I will send for you as soon as we can. I'm sorry," he said wearily as he gathered up those able to be moved.

All was silent after they left. There was no more cause for pleading. The wounded were at the mercy of this Confederate doctor. Dr. Wright and Sarah looked around at the five who remained in their care. One was bleeding profusely and probably wouldn't make it through the night, despite Dr. Wright's attention. The others would be up walking, unsteadily at best, within a few days.

"We will strive to keep you all comfortable. Do not fear. We hold no malice toward you. We are all just doing our duty," Dr. Wright explained to his involuntary guests.

Hours passed. Mary proceeded up and down the stairs, tending to the needs of the ladies and children upstairs. Peachy was in the kitchen house, cooking a thin soup of potatoes and onions from the cellar. Sarah heard her stomach growl when the smell of fresh bread drifted in the open windows.

"Take a break, Sarah. You need a rest. You've been working so hard," Dr. Wright said, pulling Sarah by her arm into the parlor. Sarah caught a glimpse of herself in a rectangular mirror. Its perfect golden frame surrounded her disheveled hair that hung down her back in tangles, and the blood and dirt that smudged her face. *My clothes need to be burned, not laundered,* she thought.

"I am a bit of a mess. Perhaps I should change my clothes and rest awhile. The worst should be over now, am I right?"

"Yes, and you have managed quite well. A finer surgeon never assisted me." Dr. Wright kissed Sarah's forehead and ushered her to the stairs.

"Well, now, if it isn't the Yankee nurse," Felicity said sarcastically, the back of her wing-backed chair turned toward Sarah as she entered her room.

"Should I have left Father to work alone?" Sarah inquired.

"I would have refused to treat those Yankee insects. It takes backbone to stand up for the Cause, Sarah. Those Yankees are the ones who killed your brother. They killed many brothers."

"And Thomas killed a lot of their brothers, too," Sarah defended.

"Alex wouldn't approve of your actions, I'm sure."

"How can you be so sure?" Sarah pressed her.

"Because, he is a Confederate officer, Sarah. He and I are a lot alike. I understand his type."

"Go on, this is getting interesting," Sarah said as she undressed.

"You wouldn't understand." Felicity closed her eyes and pretended to go to sleep.

Sarah considered all she had said. *Would Alex disapprove? Surely not.*

Sarah returned downstairs that evening feeling refreshed from her nap. She found four soldiers sleeping through their misery. The fifth had gone to his eternal resting place. Dr. Wright was sitting on the velvet settee; he was bent forward with his head resting in his hands. Through it all, he had carefully protected the settee out of concern for Mrs. Wright's feelings.

"Peachy should have our dinner ready, Papa. Would you like something to eat?" Sarah asked, putting her hand on his shoulder.

"Yes, Sarah. That would be nice." Dr. Wright never even lifted his head.

"Where is Charles?" Sarah asked about her brother when she realized he wasn't upstairs napping with the others.

"Last I saw he was sleeping on the dining room floor."

Sarah checked on her brother and found him as her father had said, asleep clutching his squirrel gun. Sarah chuckled, "What a little soldier you are, Charles."

"I needed him out there with me." Sarah spun around to find Alex propped up against the wall behind her.

"Alex! You're always sneaking up on me!" Sarah said as she embraced his filthy neck. "How did you get here? There are so many Yankees around, I was afraid for you."

"There are more around than I care for," Alex said, motioning to the sleeping men. "I was involved in a skirmish near Yellow Tavern today. From the looks of it, so were they. I decided to sneak by and make sure you were alright before I joined the other men. I guess I'll be transferring these Yanks to prison at first light."

"You will do no such thing! Not one of them is fit for travel, at least not for a few days. Father and I have done our best to patch them up, but sometimes time is what is needed," Sarah said.

"Did I understand you correctly? You and your father tended these Yankees?" Sarah could see the anger flickering in his eyes. "It is not necessary, or proper, for you to tend to the enemy as far as I'm concerned. I could just shoot them all here and now and save myself the trouble of transport. But that would be rather unpleasant for you. So, in the morning it is. I must leave now and get back to camp. I'll be back at first light with some more soldiers to help transfer these prisoners to Libbey." Alex gave Sarah a quick, hard kiss on the mouth and left.

"Was that Alex I just saw?" Dr. Wright asked, coming down the stairs with fresh clothes on.

"Mmm. Yes. He'll be back in the morning for these men." Sarah felt a twinge of disappointment.

"Well, they'll only be picking up four. This poor fellow has gone over to the other side," Dr. Wright said, covering the soldier up with a sheet.

Sam, who had slept through the entire drama, opened his eyes and looked for Sarah. With his eyes somewhat blurred, she appeared like a vision.

Staring for a brief second, Sarah blushed. She felt an amazing attraction to this Yankee. Yet, this was different from how she felt about Alex. *Alex is almost on a different plane. Alex is how life should be, how life was expected to be. Alex is up on a pedestal. Sam, he is a compelling force that makes me feel free, comfortable with who I am,* she thought.

"I guess I lived, huh?" Sam said, his voice husky with sleep. "Would you happen to have any food for this Yankee vermin?" Sarah managed to smile at Sam's playfulness. She knelt beside him with tears in her eyes as she helped him sit up. Peachy carried in a tray with soup and bread for all of them.

"A feast for kings," the others proclaimed as they woke up.

"Will you stay and talk with me, Sarah?" Sam asked as she rose to leave and join her father at the table.

"I would be glad to, Sam."

He held her hand gently, as if it were a precious gem to be treasured. Being near him brought Sarah a warm, jittery feeling. Surely Sam could hear her heart pounding fiercely! It was a pleasant feeling yet it scared her. Sarah looked into Sam's green eyes and saw that he felt what she was feeling. His eyes didn't look at her but into her, into the depths of her heart. A wave of emotion rose up within her and seemed to choke her. She felt as if her throat was closing. *How could I be feeling these things? I am betrothed to another man.* Alex was everything she had ever hoped for, yet the innocent girlish amour she had for him didn't match the intense driving force and oneness she felt with Sam.

"Thank you for your kindness. Your parents named you well, Angel of Mercy."

Shaking, Sarah backed away.

"I'm sorry, did I say something out of line, Sarah?" Sam asked quietly, reaching his hand out to her withdrawn yet close hand.

"Oh, no, it's just that, well, I," Sarah clumsily tried to think of something intelligent to say. *Maybe he's just grateful for finding a caring nurse on enemy ground,* she thought. Sarah looked into his face and knew what he meant.

Sam reached up and stroked Sarah's cheek slowly with the back of his rough, tired hand. Feeling him touch her so lovingly was almost more than she could bear.

"Well, now, I must be going. I still have quite a bit to do before I can go to sleep..." Sarah started to withdraw her hand from his tender grasp when he pulled her close and kissed her softly on the mouth.

Sarah then left without a word, with her emotions and thoughts so jumbled and her knees so wobbly she thought that surely the house was shaking.

Smiling, Peachy closed the basement door very gently, so that Sarah wouldn't know she had been watching what transpired.

CHAPTER 10

"Miss Sarah," Peachy whispered as Sarah lay in bed half-asleep.

"Peachy this is probably not good news, is it?" Sarah asked groggily.

"No'm. The men downstairs are talking about leaving tonight. Prescott and Charles standing guard on the porch isn't enough to stop them. What should we do?"

Sarah smiled inwardly at Peachy's use of "we." Sitting up and trying to think clearly, Sarah rubbed her tired head.

"Pappy say he heard tell Prichertt's runaway, John, was still around, guiding Yankees through swamps and past Confederate lines. If that be the truth, he could help these soldiers too." Peachy almost sounded hopeful that he would.

"Well, even if we were to try and help them, how on earth would we find this John fellow? It's not exactly like he hands out calling cards," Sarah whispered and bit her bottom lip as she considered the sleeping forms of Julia and Felicity.

Moving into the hallway, Peachy continued their covert discussion. "No'm. But we do know that he is still sweet on Jones' cook, Isabella. Maybe I could find out something."

"Peachy, if you are out in the middle of the night, anyone can turn you in."

"Unless I was to be travelling with my master on an urgent errand. And with soldier escort to boot," Peachy thought out loud.

"How would we get Confederate uniforms? Anyways, Confederates can spot a Federal uniform a mile away. It would be too risky."

"If you didn't notice, most of our Confederate boys don't have much in the way of uniforms anymore. Switch a few things around on them and get rid of those caps and no one will know the difference," Peachy said matter-of-factly.

"I don't know, Peachy. Alex will be here in a few hours. We don't have time to mess with this basket of snakes." Sarah looked around at her beautiful home. Even in the dark she could make out the fine, handcrafted furnishings, and the tasteful oil paintings of each of the children. She could be giving it all up, and for what? Principle?

"Peachy, I have a better idea. Go get some of my old dresses that I gave you and meet me in the basement."

Sarah and Peachy crept down the stairs to the first floor. It was obvious to Sarah that the soldiers were not asleep, although they were each laying still. Sarah walked near Sam and knelt down.

"Sarah, what are you doing?" Sam whispered.

"I'm here to help. Have your three men follow us down to the basement quietly and quickly."

Sarah led the train of freedom seekers to where Peachy waited with changes of clothes.

Sam looked at Sarah and said, "Why? You don't have to."

"It would be an awful shame for you to try to escape on your own and get caught, when I can help you just as well. Now, get dressed. Luckily your lack of food has made you all as thin as teenage girls. Make yourselves beautiful, we have a carriage ride to take by moonlight tonight."

A mad fury of tugging and pulling dresses onto their bodies ensued. Sarah and Peachy frowned at the final inspection.

"It's a good thing it's dark, that's all I can say," Sarah said as she fussed with bonnets and other camouflage. Sarah tied the bow on Sam's bonnet as he fumbled with his mangled hand. Grabbing one of the hams that they had hidden in the fireplace, Sarah brought it along with their other supplies.

"So, you did have something in hiding," Sam said just above a whisper.

"Shh! Or we'll all be as dead as this pig." Sarah shivered as they made their way to the barn, but it wasn't from the chilly Springtime air. The night owl began his infamous questioning as they walked under the tulip poplar. Sam held Sarah's hand in his gloved one.

"Maybe we'll meet again someday," Sam hoped aloud.

"Maybe." Sarah doubted that day would come.

They pulled the wagon out to the road as quietly as they were able. Prescott shouted from the shadows of the front porch, "Who is that?" trying to distinguish the females in the group.

"Just me, Prescott. These ladies need my help. Isabella is about ready to have her baby. I'm trying to leave without waking everyone. We've had such a day." Sarah sounded very confident.

"Well, be careful. Do you have your pistol?" Prescott nodded her on when she indicated she did.

The runaways jumped at every night sound on their way to the Jones' farm. What was only a four mile journey seemed to take days.

"Isabella, it's me, Peachy. Let me in." Peachy tapped lightly on Isabella's door.

Peachy was let in. For five long minutes Peachy was inside convincing Isabella of the plan. The "ladies" sat in silence, keeping guard with their eyes.

"I didn't expect you to lie for us, Sarah," Sam said.

"I didn't lie. You 'ladies' need my help. And Isabella is about to have her baby, though let's hope not tonight. So, you see, I can still maintain my integrity," Sarah explained.

"Incredible." Sarah could see his smile in the dark.

Isabella emerged, followed by Peachy. Then a large, black man appeared. *Prichertt's man, John,* Sarah concluded.

"You all will come with me now, on foot. We don't have much time 'til daylight." The tall, black man indicated for them to follow him into the woods.

"Goodbye, Sarah. Thank you." Sam pressed his lips against hers one last time as they embraced.

Putting her fingers to her lips as she watched the soldiers leave, Sarah was certain they would be in good hands.

"Now, we have a baby to deliver!" Isabella laughed, her large abdomen indicating it wouldn't be far off.

"What a shame, you were merely having false labor. We'll come back when you need us for certain." Sarah thanked Isabella and joined Peachy in the wagon.

They rode home slowly, trying to listen for any gunshots or men shouting. Only the peaceful sounds of night answered: frogs croaking in the creeks, night squirrels flying from tree to tree, and the crackle of the wagon wheels crossing over branches on the road. *The cloudy sky would prevent moonlight exposing too much,* Sarah thought gratefully. Still not certain of her motivation for her participation in the escape, Sarah didn't say a word all the way home.

Crawling back into bed, Sarah tried to catch a few moments of rest before the moment of reckoning when Alex arrived. What would she say? How would he react? Would he doubt her?

Daylight was unmerciful and swift in coming. Sarah awoke to the shouts of Alex and her father downstairs. Throwing on her dressing coat, she ran down the steps to the mass confusion below. "What is it?" Sarah asked, looking at the hysterical faces.

"They are gone! All four of them. I knew I shouldn't have trusted Prescott with such a responsibility. You've proven your worthlessness, soldier," Alex hammered away at Prescott.

"Don't blame him. You could have stayed and guarded them yourself. You knew you couldn't handle four men alone, yet you expected Prescott to keep guard all night," Dr. Wright defended his son who sat with his head buried in his mother's arms. "It's been a tiresome few days for all of us, and we are not equipped to play soldier here."

"Yes, I know. You were too busy fixing them up so they'd be good enough to escape!" Alex accused.

"I think you better go now, Corporal Brooke," Dr. Wright demanded.

Alex took them all in with a final glare. Sarah moved forward from the group. "I believe this is yours, Corporal." Handing Alex his engagement ring, Sarah said, "Goodbye, Alex."

The family watched as Alex stormed out the door and rode away without prisoners. "He'll have a grand time explaining this one." Dr. Wright couldn't help himself as he chuckled.

Felicity stared at Sarah in disbelief. "You gave up a chance of a lifetime, Sarah."

"No, I took advantage of the chance of a lifetime." Sarah went back upstairs to dress and celebrate her decision, which made more sense the longer she thought about it.

"Sarah, how was Isabella's baby?" Dr. Wright questioned Sarah after knocking softly on her door.

"False labor. Should be anytime now." Sarah avoided her father's gaze.

"Mmm. Seems to me Isabella would know false labor after six children," he pried further.

"Well, you know how it is when women get excited. A lot of times they think something is more than it really is. Am I right?"

"Indeed, Sarah, you're a very wise girl."

"One other thing, Papa. You gave Peachy to me, correct? So that would make me her master, correct?" Without waiting for the affirmative, she continued, "I would like to pursue her freedom. She can be a free servant if she would like. Is that suitable to you?"

"I think we have discovered the true Cause, don't you?" Dr. Wright smiled as he hugged Sarah and walked her down to breakfast.